# Do You Know Where Your Monster Is Tonight?

**JOANNE & DAVID WYLIE**

Monsters know the
best hiding places,
because they fit into
all sorts of spaces.

 CHILDRENS PRESS ™

CHICAGO

**Many Monster Stories** ®

Library of Congress Cataloging in Publication Data

Wylie, Joanne.
  Do you know where your monster is tonight?

  (Many monster stories)
  Summary: Monsters know good places to hide and
the reader must find the monster in each picture
as the various clocks show the hours from one to
twelve.
    1.  Children's stories, American.  [1.  Monsters—
Fiction.  2.  Time—Fiction]  I.  Wylie, David (David
Graham)  II.  Title.  III.  Series.
PZ7.W9775Do  1984    [E]       84-12122
ISBN 0-516-04491-5          AACR2

# Do
# You Know
# Where Your
# Monster Is
# Tonight?

JOANNE & DAVID WYLIE

It's ONE o'clock.

Let's look for him.

It's TWO o'clock.

Keep on looking.

It's THREE o'clock.

He must be somewhere.

It's FOUR o'clock.

You know he's here.

It's FIVE o'clock.

Where can he be?

It's SIX o'clock.

Okay monster, where are you?

It's SEVEN o'clock.

He wouldn't just disappear.

It's EIGHT o'clock.

Don't you see him?

It's NINE o'clock.

Come out, come out, wherever you are.

It's TEN o'clock.

Don't give up.

It's ELEVEN o'clock.

Do you need help?

It's TWELVE o'clock.

MIDNIGHT or NOON,
    I sure hope you find him soon.

You found him.

Time flies when you're having fun.

Where do you like to hide?

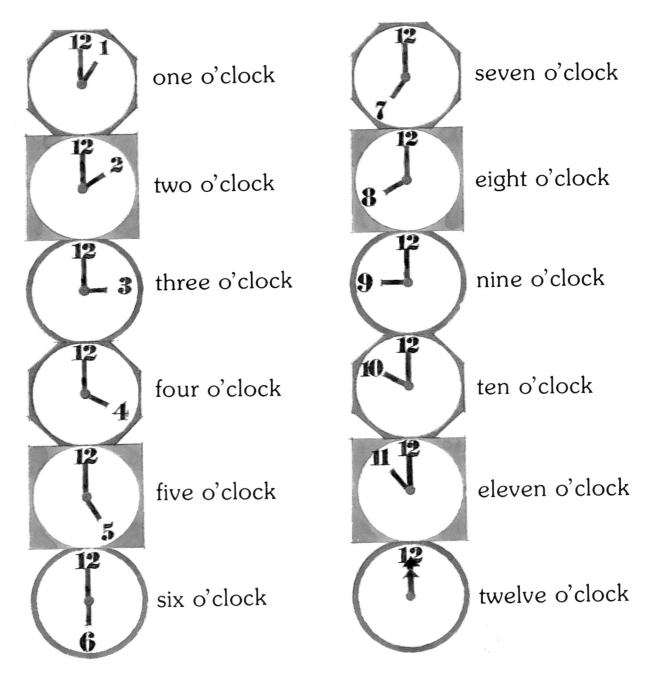

one o'clock

two o'clock

three o'clock

four o'clock

five o'clock

six o'clock

seven o'clock

eight o'clock

nine o'clock

ten o'clock

eleven o'clock

twelve o'clock